Loving You Is Easy Poetry

(Quick Read Poems Series)

By Mini Celection Williams

Cover Art by Cassandra A. Williams

CHAPTER ONE

<u>He Loves Me and I Love Him, So We Talk About Our Future Together</u>

He loves me and I love him, so we talk about our future together.

We been together for years, so our relationship has weathered the stormy weathers.

His touch caresses me all over like a soft feather.

And when he kisses me all my thought's scatters.

He loves me and I love him, so we talk about our future together.

When he looks me in my eyes and hold my hands to his lips nothing seems to matter.

His silly faces and animated voice always make me do a deep belly laughter.

And when its time to bed what comes after makes me wetter and wetter.

He loves me and I love him, so we talk about our future together.

Executing each step to build a life that will only get better and better.

Every time we conduct a goal we celebrate with friends and cater.

While the excitement builds to love on one another later.

He loves me and I love him, so we talk about our future together.

He shares his dream and goal of one day becoming a father.

And I joke while him about if that come not wanting to get fatter.

He looked me in my eyes and said my beauty will show in our daughter.

He loves me and I love him, so we talk about our future together.

Once he set his mind on something he is a go getter.

So, when he said he want a child he wants stop until he meets her.

I cannot help smiling as we talk about our future together.

CHAPTER TWO

<u>I Am Scared as I Hold My First Pregnancy Test</u>

I am scared as I hold my first pregnancy test.

Wondering which result will be best.

As I stand in front of the bathroom toilet gripping this test.

Knowing that my child's father will do his best.

I am scared as I hold my first pregnancy test.

Nervous and praying to God because of the stress.

Even though it would be all over if I just take the test.

But dragging it out I have found comfort in the stress.

I am scared as I hold my first pregnancy test.

Doubting my decision in baby making when I said yes.

My hands are now sweating as I am gripping the test.

Never knew how life changing one word could be… yes.

I am scared as I hold my first pregnancy test.

Being a coward as I just stand here and guess.

Hearing my husband praying I know its time I take the test.

Feeling his different emotions as he too tries to give his best guess.

I am scared as I hold my first pregnancy test.

Waiting on the result not sure if it will be no or yes.

Feeling my significant other behind me so we both know the results of the test.

Shook when we see a no instead of the expected yes.

CHAPTER THREE

<u>Watching The Disappointment Crosses His Handsome Face</u>

Watching the disappointment crosses his handsome face.

Makes me ashamed that I put too much in my period being late.

Because it is now hard for me to look him in his face.

I watch him walk away as he says he will be home late.

Watching the disappointment crosses his handsome face.

I found myself that evening alone as I ate.

Wishing my love were across from me as we converse face to face.

As much as I had no appetite I still sat here quietly and ate.

Watching the disappointment crosses his handsome face.

I had no choice but to respect his need for space.

Going to bed alone with uncontrollable tears streaming down my face.

Hoping that we come together and fill this empty space.

Watching the disappointment crosses his handsome face.

Knowing that I cannot rush how a person feel and that I must move at his pace.

But I would give anything to see a smile stretch across his face.

And I miss the way we made love at our own pace.

Watching the disappointment crosses his handsome face.

I am for once speechless and unsure of what to say.

But I am having doubts about us and not sure if it shows on my face.

However, the moment he walks up and kiss me I know exactly what to say.

CHAPTER FOUR

<u>We Express Our Feelings aloud to One Another</u>

We express our feelings aloud to one another.

And I express my eagerness now to becoming a mother.

And how we may have difficulties, but it will not separate us farther.

I kiss and tell him how he will make an excellent father.

We express our feelings aloud to one another.

We talk about our support team with our own mothers.

While laughing and talking about my silly brothers.

Or the strict upbringings of both of our fathers.

We express our feelings aloud to one another.

We both wanted a son first so he can be a protective older brother.

Our children will be close and will always confine in one another.

Not precise on their shade, eyes, or hair color.

We express our feelings aloud to one another.

As the feeling of peace wash over me no longer bother.

Never wanting to be in that space where we were far away from one another.

Instead, we face all storms with each other.

We express our feelings aloud to one another

We know the insecurities and childhood traumas with our fathers and mothers.

So, they made the changes to be better for him or her.

Their household will be of peace, love, honor, and respect with each other.

CHAPTER FIVE

<u>Date night with my other half was a blast.</u>

Date night with my other half was a blast.

It was well throughout, and he did not have to spend any cash.

He had extra special moments in them from the beginning of our past.

It is always the trivial things for me even when others may think its trash.

Date night with my other half was a blast.

And I love how slow time went and the special moments had last.

Even when we were intimate, he stopped me and told me there was no need to go fast.

He knows the moans he will get when he slaps my ass.

Date night with my other half was a blast.

At one point I was curled up next to him as we both watched the Flash.

I love when he whispers my nickname, "Cass."

He always says I look sexy with a dash of class.

Date night with my other half was a blast.

As we talked about topics with no relevance while we laugh.

We did not finish or bottle of wine nor what was still left in our glass.

Instead made out while prayed I did not pass gas.

Date night with my other half was a blast.

I felt his hand going up my back to unfasten my bra fast.

Loving the way this man oversees every task.

Especially the perfect way he rubs and smack my ass.

CHAPTER SIX

<u>I Cannot Believe This Happening to Me.</u>

I cannot believe this is happening to me.

As the doctors told me that in eight months you will be with me.

But that was not true as I miscarried and felt the pain as you left me.

There was nothing to do but cry, pray and ask why you were taking from me.

I cannot believe this is happening to me.

Knowing that when I wake up tomorrow you will no longer be inside me.

We were one and now there is no we but only me.

People stay asking what they can do but there is no way to comfort me.

I cannot believe this is happening to me.

To be honest I just want everyone stay away from me.

No one understands what I am going through but me.

I hate the sympathy and those who say they can relate to me.

I cannot believe this happening to me.

The one I knew without a doubt love me for me.

For an unknown reason was taken from me.

While I contracted and my child spilled out it took a part of me.

I cannot believe this happening to me.

I no longer fill whole and I no longer feel like me.

Without a doubt I knew he or she would have brought out the best in me.

But my body is not mine, my spirit is broken, and I cannot connect to me.

CHAPTER SEVEN

<u>My Tears of Sorrow Will not Promise Me Tomorrow, As I Hold You in My Arms</u>

My tears of sorrow will not promise me tomorrow, as I hold you in my arms.

What kind of mother am I when I had promise you no harm?

What did I do wrong to give birth to a stillborn?

Kissing your forehead but not feeling the welcoming warmth.

My tears of sorrow will not promise me tomorrow, as I hold you in my arms.

Not wanting to let go of you as the nurse reach out instead, I hold you firm.

Not wanting to accept it in my heart and not wanting it to be real that I had to mourn.

That life had robbed me of all experiences before you were born.

My tears of sorrow will not promise me tomorrow, as I hold you in my arms.

I question why life will not allow me to have a child alive when its born.

Miscarriages and stillborn has me sick, tired, and fed up with each passing year to mourn.

Not sure if I can go through this again but wanting a child so I am so torn.

My tears of sorrow will not promise me tomorrow, as I hold you in my arms.

Questioning why the Most high would not have you crying when you were born.

I wanted the chance to watch you as you lay on my underarms.

To enjoy falling asleep until we hear my husband's phone alarm.

My tears of sorrow will not promise me tomorrow, as I hold you in my arms.

I was just as excited as everyone as the date drew never for my baby to be born.

Never in my widest dream did I imagine when I delivered it would be stillborn.

You came out and the sight of you was breathtaking mix with pride as I mourn.

CHAPTER EIGHT

Fear Grips Me of Going Through This Pain Again

Fear grips me of going through this pain again.

Nervous as he wants to be intimate again.

I love him and I miss him, but I cannot go through it again.

I keep seeing my child's face over again.

Fear grips me of going through this pain again.

He looks me in my eyes and tell me he loves me again.

And that when I am ready, we can try again.

But the heartache and pain are repeating again.

Fear grips me of going through this pain again.

Everyone feels as though I will lose him this time if I give up again.

Hearing those words speaks fear in me again.

Because I know this love is only once and would never be explored again.

Fear grips me of going through this again.

I cancelled another date night again.

Scared that he will want to have sex again.

But I never want to see another tiny dead face again.

Fear grips me of going through this again.

Crying on our bathroom floors again.

Going through the motions of the day again.

Seeing him look lonely I want to hold him again.

Fear grips me of going through this again.

Once more I feel like I am losing my best friend again.

As always when I feel like I am going over the deep end again.

My husband pulls me out and comforts me again.

CHAPTER NINE

<u>His Unconditional Love and Patience Have Me Ready to Give Life A Chance</u>

His unconditional love and patience have me ready to give life a chance.

As we communicate to teach one another again.

On our anniversary our favorite song played while we dance.

My body tangled all over as my husband held my hand.

His unconditional love and patience have me ready to give life a chance.

The more we do the closer we become and the need to have a son is strong.

I cannot wait to see how our child will look like me or my man.

For me, the doubt is in the wait and how the months are long.

His unconditional love and patience have me ready to give life a chance.

He truly is my other half in all ways and picks up where I am not strong.

I am so lucky that I was favored to be bless with this extraordinary man.

And I pray that the days, months, and years together will be long.

His unconditional love and patience have me ready to give life a chance.

We balance one another with our way of thinking, living, and speaking.

Something about his makes my legs weak and stomach fluttery with one glance.

And when he is not around, as though something is missing.

His unconditional love and patience have me ready to give life a chance.

Not sure what life has in store for me, but I am ready to try again.

Thoughts of how he holds and guides me as we dance.

Happy that no matter what we face in life we will get through it hand in hand.

CHAPTER TEN

<u>Nine Months Later You Are Here</u>

Nine months later you are here.

Holding you in my arms has now cancelled out any fear.

A smile is on my face as I watch your father asleep in the chair.

But the tide of emotions is collected in this one tear.

Nine months later you are here.

The first time I heard your cries was music to my ears.

Knowing my baby was born alive and breathing in air.

I drifted off to a comfortable sleep knowing you was near.

Nine months later you are here.

The purpose of all my past pains is now clear.

And the moment I gave into faith you had appeared.

Without a doubt I have to say this is my favorite year.

Nine months later you are here.

Pains of the earlier loss of the past years.

Had me experiencing hurt that was unbelievably severe.

At the time when all of this would end was unclear.

Nine months later you are here.

Holding you tight in my arms I whisper my love in your ear.

Wanting you to grow up with happiness and peace with no fear.

My hopes for you and your future I shed with this one tear.

This is dedicated to anyone who has experienced any of this. Or to anyone who see someone go through any of this. Our words can be healing but it can also be pain.

You can check out more poetry and short storis by Mini Celection Williams.

The release will be in July 2022.

You can follow me on social media platforms or google me @Mini Celection Williams.

And do not forget to look for my eBooks on all platforms and soon paperback books will be available as well.

Thank you for joining me on this exciting journey of writing.

Mini Celection Williams is a SHORT STORY (under 10,000 words) author from the Show-Me State. She is a daughter, mother, sister, aunt, Mee-maw, and businessperson. She has an imagination that is unique and a bit different from others. And because of that, she wants to share it with you all. Come join her in her world of writing as she explores different topics.